W9-ATF-038

DATE DUE			

Abby's Asthma and the Big Race

Theresa Martin Golding

Illustrated by Margeaux Lucas

Albert Whitman & Company, Morton Grove, Illinois

To Mary Kathryn, who knows how to win the race.—TG

For the irrepressible Yvonne Colebank.—ML

Library of Congress Cataloging-in-Publication Data

Golding, Theresa Martin.
Abby's asthma and the big race / by Theresa Martin Golding ;
illustrated by Margeaux Lucas.
p. cm.
Summary: Abby is practicing for the big race,
but she is worried that her asthma will stop her from winning.
ISBN 978-0-8075-0465-9
[1. Asthma—Fiction. 2. Racing—Fiction.] I. Lucas, Margeaux, ill. II. Title.
PZ7.G56775Ab 2009 [E]—dc22 2008028084

The design is by Carol Gildar.

For more information about Albert Whitman & Company,
visit our web site at www.albertwhitman.com.

Abby's legs were long and fast,
but sometimes her breath was short.

At school, Colin's goal for the year was to become a better reader.

Emily wanted an *A* in math.

Then it was Abby's turn to read her paper.

She took a deep breath, as deep as she could. "This year my goal is to run in the big race at the fair. And I think I am fast enough to win."

Jason's eyes grew wide. Emily sat forward in her seat.

"Abby *is* very fast," Devin said.

"But doesn't she have asthma?" asked Hari. "How can she win the race?"

Miss Lilly whispered in Abby's ear. "The pie-eating contest is fun, too," she said.

At recess, Abby played with Elana on the swings. Jason ran past, calling, "Abby! Abby! She's no fun! She swings like a baby and she can't run!"

Abby jumped off the swing. "I *am* going to run in the big race this year," she shouted after Jason. "Just you wait and see how fast I will be!"

After school, Abby ran home, over the hill and through the field. The air was warm and dusty. "Abby!" Dad cried. "What's wrong?"

"I'm…practicing…for…the…big…race," she wheezed.

Inside, Abby took two puffs of her inhaler. Her dad fixed her a snack. "It's a bad allergy day today," he said. "Lots of pollen in the air."

Abby popped three cookies in her mouth. "I hope there's not too much pollen on the day of the big race," she mumbled.

Dad laughed at Abby's stuffed cheeks. "I think you would be good at the pie-eating contest, too!" he said.

One day, everyone was bundled up for gym class. They played soccer in the sharp, cold air. Frost glittered in the branches of the bare trees. Jason ran past. "Abby! Abby! She's no fun! She can't play soccer 'cause girls can't run," he sang.

Abby sped toward Jason.
She stole the ball from him and
scored a goal. Elana and Devin
threw their arms around Abby.
"The girls win!" they cheered.

Back in the warm classroom, Abby's chest was tight.
Air couldn't go in and air couldn't get out.
Jason stared. "Miss Lilly," he cried. "I think
Abby is having an asthma attack!"

Miss Lilly rushed Abby to the nurse's office.

Abby took two puffs of her inhaler. She knew how to stay calm and to count as she breathed slowly in and out.

"You're doing fine now," Nurse Bonner said.

"Did you know that I'm going to run in the big race this year?" Abby asked.

"My favorite event is the pie-eating contest," Nurse Bonner said. "If you change your mind about running, maybe you could try that."

Mom took Abby to her appointment with the asthma doctor. Abby blew hard into the spirometer, the machine that measured her breathing.

Doctor Allison watched the numbers come up on the computer screen. "You're doing really well, Abby," she said.

"I'm going to run in the big race this year, Dr. Allison," Abby said. "And I'm fast. I think I could win."

Dr. Allison listened to Abby's chest with her stethoscope. "Go for it, Abby!" she said. "Just remember to keep taking your medicine every day and to warm up before the race."

Each night before bed, Abby did the breathing exercises that the doctor had taught her. Twice a day she blew into her peak flow meter and wrote down the numbers in her chart.

And every week Abby went with her dad to the health club.
She ran on the treadmill while Dad lifted his weights.

One day the air in the exercise room felt warm and stuffy, and Abby could smell a lady's strong perfume. She coughed and wheezed when she tried to run. She had to stop. Abby slumped in a chair and waited for Dad.

"What's the matter, Abby?" asked Todd, the trainer.

"I wanted to win the big race this year." Abby sighed. "But I might enter the pie-eating contest instead. Everyone says that it's fun."

The next week when Abby went to the health club,
there was a ribbon hanging in front of the treadmill. Todd
smiled. "Pretend this is the finish line. Go for it, Abby!"

Abby warmed up. Then she ran hard. She might not win, but at least she would try her best to finish the race.

Week after week Abby ran, practicing hard.

At last, the day of the fair arrived. Abby passed right by the merry-go-round and the pie-eating contest. She was going to sign up for the big race!

At the race booth, a lady pinned a number to Abby's shirt. Abby's legs were shaky, and it felt as though butterflies were dancing in her stomach.

She stretched and ran her warm-up sprints.
Fifteen minutes before race time, she took two
puffs of her inhaler.

The runners all stood at the starting line.

"Good luck, Abby!" Mom called.

Jason pushed his way to the front. Abby looked straight ahead.

"On your marks, get set, GO!" shouted the starter. Abby ran.

She flew by Elana and Hari. Emily tried hard but couldn't keep up. Only Jason was ahead of Abby. She raced faster, her hair flying in the wind. She saw the ribbon stretched across the finish line.

Her heart was pounding, but she took good, deep breaths, just as she had practiced. She pushed herself forward and broke the ribbon.

"Abby wins!" shouted the official.

Abby won the first-place ribbon and a big blueberry pie, which she shared with Miss Lilly, her mom and dad, and her friends.

"Congratulations," Jason said. "You won the big race. You really *are* the fastest!"

"Yes," Abby giggled, "I did win, but eating pie with my friends is fun, too."

"Can I have the last piece of pie?" Jason asked.

"I'll race you for it!" Abby called. With a good, deep breath, she was off and running again.

Asthma and Exercise

Asthma is a chronic condition in which swollen and inflamed airways in the lungs lead to breathing problems known as "attacks." These include symptoms like coughing, wheezing, chest tightness, and shortness of breath. Attacks happen when the airways overreact to certain triggers, such as physical activity, allergens, and irritants like smoke and cold air. With proper medication and the help of a physician, a child can control his or her asthma and learn to avoid triggers.

Of course, kids want to be physically active—and they should be, even with asthma. Warming up can reduce symptoms, and using a quick-relieving inhaler fifteen minutes before exercise will help airway muscles relax. The warm-up can include breathing exercises, such as sitting up straight while taking long deep breaths through the nose and exhaling through the mouth.

It's important to monitor changes in asthma symptoms, too. Some people use a peak flow meter to measure how well their lungs are working, and a low reading on the meter can indicate an approaching attack. Long-term preventive medication may be taken daily as well.

When children are diagnosed with asthma, their parents often panic. They worry that their children will not be able to do sports or even play outside. But that's usually far from the truth: with rare exceptions, asthma will not limit physical activity. In fact, there are world class athletes with asthma in almost every sport. To give you a sense of how common and manageable asthma is in the world of sports, about 10 percent of the members of recent United States Olympic teams have asthma—compared to just 5 percent of people in the U.S. in general!

Jonathan M. Spergel, M.D., Ph.D.
Associate Professor of Pediatrics
Chief, Allergy Section
The Children's Hospital of Philadelphia